"I don't think Becky would want me along," I said.

Becky whispered something in Chris's ear. I hate people telling secrets in front of me. It always makes me feel they're whispering about me, and in Becky's case, I was positive that I was right.

Chris shrugged. He smiled a little sheepishly at me.

"What's the matter, Becky?" I asked. "Don't you want company? Don't worry, I couldn't care less about the stupid commando raids."

Becky laughed at me. "That's just because you've never played the game."

"Right," teased Cindi. "It's time to get down and dirty, Darlene."

I laughed. I knew Cindi wasn't talking about the commando raids. Well, if it was a fight Becky wanted, I wasn't going to back off.

**Look for these and other books
in THE GYMNASTS series:**

THE GYMNASTS

#17 GYMNAST COMMANDOS

Elizabeth Levy

AN
APPLE
PAPERBACK

SCHOLASTIC INC.
New York Toronto London Auckland Sydney

To Camp Killooleet —
home of the original commando game

ISBN 0-590-43835-2

Copyright © 1991 by Elizabeth Levy. All rights reserved. Published by Scholastic Inc. APPLE PAPERBACKS is a registered trademark of Scholastic Inc. THE GYMNASTS is a trademark of Scholastic Inc.

12 11 10 9 8 7 6 5 4 3 2 1   1 2 3 4 5 6/9

Printed in the U.S.A.   40

First Scholastic printing, May 1991

Big Beef and
the Pinecones

I couldn't believe my eyes. The brochure was sitting on our dining room table. It had a picture of my dad on the cover with his football helmet off and his Broncos uniform with the number 17 in orange and black.

The brochure showed some kids playing tennis in one corner, a very pretty girl on horseback in another, and a bunch of boys playing football in the far left. The only problem was that as far as I knew, my dad wasn't going to any camp except the Denver Broncos training camp toward the end of July. He's one of the oldest players on the team, and I know that each year it gets harder and harder for him to keep in shape.

"Dad, what's this?" I yelled. I had just come

home from gymnastics. It was hot, and the Evergreen Gymnastics Academy isn't air-conditioned. Anybody who thinks it doesn't get hot in Denver because we're called the Mile High City hasn't been there during a heat wave. And it was only early June.

Dad walked into the dining room. "What do you think?" he asked me, pointing to the brochure in my hand.

"Is it a joke?" I asked.

Dad looked hurt. "No," he said. He took the brochure from me. "You know my friend Sweet Willie. On the field he was the meanest defensive back for Oakland. But off it, he was the sweetest guy in the world. He started a sports camp. He asked me to be a special guest this year. I'm going up for the first two weeks of July, before training camp starts."

"Is this a camp just for football players?" I asked. "It's got girls on the cover."

"It's co-ed. It attracts kids from all different sports, not just football, but track and field, tennis, even gymnastics. It's got a gym in a tent."

"I can't imagine a gym in a tent."

"It'll be cool. The oldest campers are around your age, thirteen and fourteen. I thought it would be kind of fun if we all went together," said Dad. "They've invited Mom and your little sisters to stay with me in the Main House. But you would be a camper. I would have told you sooner, but the deal wasn't final. I didn't want you to get your hopes up."

I made a face. I couldn't help myself. Don't get me wrong, I love my mom and dad. It's just that I get very tired of always being "Big Beef's daughter." When I go to football games, I have to dress nicely because I know the TV cameras are going to zero in on Mom and me every time Dad gets tackled. Whenever I meet a new kid, they always want to know more about my dad than about me. It used to be just boys, but lately it seems girls are just as into football as some of the boys.

One of the reasons I love my own gym, and my coach Patrick, is that nobody there makes a big deal about my dad. My teammates are terrific about it. I think it's because gymnastics is so different from football. But any camp with my dad's picture on the brochure had to have a lot of football nuts.

Dad didn't like the expression on my face. "Darlene," he said, "you know I'm nearing retirement age. I've got to think about our future, about my life after football. And I love kids. I've always wanted to coach."

"I know," I admitted. I think my dad would make a great coach someday. It's funny, though — as much as I get embarrassed by being his daughter, I know I will miss the fame when he finally stops playing football professionally.

"Besides," said Dad, "do you know where this camp is?"

"No," I said. "I just looked at the cover."

"Woody Creek, Colorado, about five hours from Denver. It's in the Rockies ten miles outside Aspen. It's about twenty degrees cooler than Denver. They've got white-water rafting, an Olympic-size swimming pool, horseback riding . . ."

Dad knows that I love to ride. "Cindi loves horses, too," I said.

Cindi Jockett is one of the six Pinecones, my team. We're very tight. Cindi, Lauren Baca, and Jodi Sutton, and I all started at Patrick's gym together. They were the first kids I ever met who treated me like a normal being instead of a freak because my dad is famous.

"I've been thinking of the Pinecones," said Dad. "I knew you wouldn't want to leave them behind. I can get them a special discount at the camp so it won't be too expensive."

I grinned at Dad. "You really want me to go, don't you?" I asked.

Dad nodded. "If this summer's a success, Sweet Willie has somebody interested in investing in a string of sports camps all over the country. But I don't want to get involved in anything until I really see what it's like."

I flipped through the brochure. It looked great. The kids were all smiling. The photographs showed pine and aspen forests, bright petunias and pansies planted around the swimming pool, and kids squirting each other with water guns.

"I'll tell the Pinecones about it," I promised.

Dad was smiling.

"What are you grinning about?" I asked. I knew he was positive that the Pinecones would jump at the chance to go to his camp. And he was right.

"I'm just daydreaming," said Dad. "You know I love my daydreams. Big Beef and the Pinecones. It's a winning combination."

"It sounds like a dinner special," I teased him.

Training in Being Cross

Our locker rooms at the Evergreen Gymnastics Academy are anything but luxurious. The walls are cinder blocks painted light green, and there are just a couple of benches and dark green lockers. Still, it's one of my favorite places in the world and *the* place where we do most of our talking.

"It's an all-around sports camp," I explained to my teammates. "I really don't know much about it, except Dad says it's got a good reputation. And he says that if all the Pinecones want to go, he can get us a special discount."

"I like the fact that it's not a gymnastics camp," said Jodi. "I never wanted to go to one of those camps. I think it would be boring to be around gymnasts all the time." That's funny coming from Jodi. She comes from a family that really takes gymnastics seriously. Jodi's parents are divorced. Her dad lives in St. Louis, and he owns his own gymnastics academy. Jodi's mom got remarried a while ago. We all went to the wedding. She was the coach of the boys' team until she had a baby recently. She's taking a break.

"I went to a gymnastics camp once," said Ashley Frank. Ashley is the only Pinecone who is something of a pill. She's young — only nine — and she's got potential. I don't just mean as a gymnast; I mean as a human being, too. Every once in a while she shows signs of being a real one. Ashley can be okay, but then she reverts to whining, and when she whines she's a pain.

"I think it sounds neat," said Cindi.

"It's a proven fact that the kids who go to one of these camps really improve," said Lauren. "We can do lots of cross-training," she added. "You know. It's all the rage in sports now. To get better at running, you lift weights." Lauren always says "It's a proven fact." When I first met her, I thought she was a little too smart, but now I know that she's smart and funny.

"Can I see that brochure?" asked Heidi. Heidi Ferguson is not actually a Pinecone. She's fourteen. The idea of Heidi being a Pinecone is almost a joke. Heidi Ferguson is one of the best gymnasts in the world *when* she's got her head screwed on right. That isn't all the time. Heidi almost quit gymnastics completely. She has anorexia, and I think she had a nervous breakdown, although nobody called it that officially. Then she started working out casually at our gym. Patrick says that we're good for Heidi because we're teaching her that gymnastics can be fun again. I like her. I have to admit that I like her brother Chris even more. He's a freestyle skier, and unfortunately he has to spend most of his time in Lake Placid, New York, training. It's a long way from the Mile High City. I haven't seen him in quite a while.

"Would you be interested?" I asked Heidi. I think of Heidi as so single-minded that it's hard to imagine her at anything else but a dedicated gymnastics camp.

Heidi grinned. "I like the idea of its being co-ed. And Dr. Joe, my shrink, wants me to be more well-rounded. Besides, Lauren's right. Cross-training is all the rage now, even for gymnasts. I wouldn't mind doing a little mountain biking. I'm not sure about getting on a horse."

"I don't get it," said Ti An Truong. Ti An's the tiniest Pinecone, and she's a lot sweeter and nicer than Ashley. And she's also a terrific gymnast. She just needs a little more confidence.

"What's cross-training? Who needs training in being cross?"

"Becky Dyson," snorted Cindi in a half-whisper. Becky was across the locker room, and she looked up when she heard her name. Becky Dyson is really one nasty piece of work. I keep looking for some redeeming quality in her. I figure anybody that snotty has to be hurting inside. But Becky just seems to be rotten through and through. She's a good gymnast, though not nearly as good as Heidi.

"Cross-training just means doing different sports to keep in shape," explained Heidi to Ti An. "It exercises different parts of your body."

"I think Darlene is already a little cross about this sports camp," said Ti An. "You don't really want to go, do you, Darlene?"

I looked down at Ti An. She's just a little kid, but I forget how much she notices. I smiled at her. "I'm not really cross," I explained. "I'm just worried that everybody at this camp will expect me to be this supermacho girl, just 'cause my dad is a football player."

"Yo, macho!" hooted Becky. "How many trunks of clothes are you going to bring?"

Everybody knows that I do love clothes and style. My mom used to be a fashion model full time, and she still does some modeling part time.

"What does it matter to you?" I shouted to Becky. I've learned a lot about bullies from my dad. You can't let them get away with snide remarks. If you call her bluff, nine times out of ten, a bully will back down.

Unfortunately this was one of the tenth times. Becky took five steps into the middle of the locker room and stuck her face close to mine.

"It just so happens that I've already signed up for that sports camp," she said. "I went last year. I think it's the best camp in the world. I just got a letter that your father was going to be the featured guest this summer. Wait till you go on one of the commando raids. Somehow I never pictured you in camouflage."

"What commando raids?" I asked her.

Becky sneered. "This isn't a camp for sissy Pinecones."

Cindi pulled my arm. Lauren, Jodi, and Ti An gestured to me from the corner of the locker room. Cindi guided me over to them.

"Don't give Becky the satisfaction of knowing more than you do about this camp," said Lauren. "We can find out all about these so-called commandos from your dad."

I sighed. "I can't believe our bad luck. Becky's going to this camp."

We walked out into the gym. It was sweltering already, and we hadn't even begun to work out.

We did our warm-ups. Patrick was ready for us by the tumbling mats where we were practicing the level six floor routine.

"Patrick!" said Lauren, excitedly. Lauren can never wait to tell Patrick anything. "Did you hear that Big Beef invited all of us to this neat sports camp in the Rocky Mountains near Aspen?"

"It's not a gymnastics camp," I explained to Patrick. I thought maybe he wouldn't want us to go if we weren't going to be really working on gymnastics.

"It sounds like a great opportunity," said Patrick. "You kids could use a break."

"They've got some kind of tent for gymnastics," I said, "but I don't think it's a big deal up there."

"That's okay," said Patrick. "You should just relax, don't worry about concentrating on gymnastics. Remember, some of the best athletes in the world are better after taking a break. It would be a good chance to keep up your fitness and do some cross-training."

"That's what I thought," said Jodi.

"Apparently Becky's gone to this camp before," I said. "She says it's great."

"Personally," said Ti An, "I don't think Becky needs any more training in being cross."

You've gotta like Ti An.

3

It'll Be a Hoot

I told Dad at dinner that the Pinecones were interested in going to camp.

"Terrific," said Dad. "I'll call all their parents right away."

"What's this about playing commandos?" I asked.

"All I can tell you is that Sweet Willie told me that they have a great game that the campers all love."

"Commando raids?" asked Mom, a little suspiciously.

"It's just a game," said Dad, "kind of like color war."

"Becky Dyson went last year," I said. "She said it's the best camp in the world."

"Well, *that's* a good recommendation," said Mom, sounding amused. She knows how I feel about Becky.

I made a face.

"Darlene hates Becky," piped up my sister Debi, who's four years old.

"Hate is too strong a word," I said. "Let's just say she's a major pain in the neck."

"You call *me* a pain in the neck," said Debi.

"Yeah, but you are a minor pain in the neck," I explained. "Most of the time." Actually my little sisters, Debi and Deirdre, are pretty cute. Mom had me when she was real young, and then she waited a while to have Debi and Deirdre.

The phone rang. "I'll get it," I said.

"Let the machine answer it," said Dad. "Let's finish dinner."

Our answering machine is in the kitchen. The ringing stopped. Then I heard a voice. "Uh . . . Hi, Mr. and Mrs. Broderick. This is for Darlene. Hi . . . Darlene . . . I'm in Lake Placid . . . but . . ."

"It's Chris!" I said, jumping up. I knocked over a glass of water.

"Darlene!" said Dad.

"Go," said Mom. "I'll mop it up."

"Darlene isn't supposed to get up from the table," said Debi.

"You are a *major* pain in the neck sometimes," I snapped.

"Go, quick, before he hangs up," said Mom, continuing to dab at the water with her napkin as it dribbled onto Dad's lap.

I ran into the kitchen and grabbed the phone just as Chris was about to hang up.

"Chris!" I said. I knew I sounded out of breath.

"Darlene, is that you? Not a machine?"

I sank down into a big easy chair that we keep near the phone in the kitchen. "It's me," I said, trying to stop gulping for breath. I didn't want Chris to think I was too excited by the fact that he called.

"I hate machines," said Chris. I hadn't heard from Chris in quite a while. He lives in a dorm and doesn't have a private phone. Besides, long-distance calls are expensive, and he's not great at writing.

"How's it going?" I asked him. What a stupid question.

"Well, I've mastered a double twist," he said. "I'm doing better at that than at the schoolwork. The coach here takes school very seriously. He wants us all to win college scholarships. I'd rather just ski."

"Dad always says that teenage athletes have

14

got to take school seriously, 'cause one injury can blow you away." I wished I hadn't said that. I sounded like such a goody-goody.

"Yeah, I know," said Chris. "Still, I'd *rather* major in double twists."

"I can't even do a double twist on the floor yet," I admitted.

"Well, remember, I start with the advantage of being four stories off the ground when I take off the ski jump."

"But you're also wearing six-foot skis on your feet while you're twisting." I couldn't believe that we were wasting time long distance talking about double twists.

"Anyhow, I'm calling about something much more fun than either school or double twists," said Chris.

"Oh, yeah?" I teased. "What could be more fun than that?"

"Heidi told me that your dad is going to be running a sports camp in the Rockies near Aspen."

"Not exactly running it, but he's going to be the guest athlete," I said.

"Heidi wants to go. Her doctors think it would be good for her. She really does love hanging out with the Pinecones. You make her laugh. I used to be the only person in the world who could make Heidi laugh."

"She's good for all of us, too," I admitted. "It's hard to goof around in the gym when Heidi's around."

"You're going to the sports camp, aren't you?" asked Chris.

"I guess so," I said. "Everybody wants me to go."

"Well, I hope you go, 'cause I think I talked my coach and my folks into letting me come out for a couple of weeks in July. He's heard of this camp. It's supposed to be terrific. He thinks it will be great cross-training for me. Besides, one of the kids here told me about the commando games that they play at that camp. It'll be a hoot."

I was biting my lower lip, something I do when I'm nervous. I couldn't believe that Chris was actually coming west to go to the camp. Two whole weeks together. Except Chris sounded more excited about the commando games than about us being together.

"Right, it'll be a hoot. Do you know exactly what these commando raids are?" I asked him.

"No," admitted Chris, "but I know they're going to be fun."

"Me, too," I said. I could hear somebody yelling at Chris on his end.

"Somebody needs the phone," he said. "I've got to go."

16

"Okay," I said, but I kind of wished we could have talked longer.

I hung up and went back into the dining room. "Darlene talked to her boyfriend. Darlene talked to her boyfriend," taunted Debi.

"He's not my boyfriend," I said.

"I should hope not," said Dad. "Thirteen is too young to have a steady boyfriend."

"Dad, he spends most of his time two thousand miles away," I said.

"What did he want?" Mom asked.

"He and Heidi both want to go to the sports camp," I said, chewing on my lower lip.

Dad rolled his eyes.

"I think that'll be nice," said Mom.

"Darlene and Chris . . . Darlene and Chris," chanted Debi.

"Shut up," I muttered.

"Darlene," Mom warned me. I apologized, but I didn't mean it. I didn't like being teased about Chris, and I was afraid I was going to get a lot more of it, and not just from my little sister.

4

No Cat Fights, Please

On the day we were leaving for camp, we had to be at the bus terminal at eight in the morning. I am not an early morning person. I hadn't heard from Chris since his phone call. I knew he was coming because Heidi had told me, but he hadn't bothered to call and tell me that it was for sure.

At the bus terminal, there was an incredible amount of sports gear lined up at the baggage counter. It made me feel good that I had managed to pack my stuff into only two suitcases. All the Pinecones' folks had come to see us off: Jodi's mom with her new baby and Barking Barney, her husband; the Bacas; Cindi's brothers and mom and dad. It was quite a scene. Finally the parents were asked to leave so that we could get organized to board the bus.

That's when it really started to get lively. Kids shrieked with joy to see each other again. We Pinecones stood out because nobody knew us. Some of the campers made us gymnasts look like midgets. I'm tall for a gymnast, but there were some boys who had to be younger than I am who were really muscular and big.

"I think we're in the land of giants," whispered Lauren, who is short for eleven years old. "Look at the size of that kid." She kind of gestured with her chin to a boy who looked like he weighed about one hundred and fifty pounds, and he was all muscle. He had a baby face, and he didn't look much older than twelve.

"He's got to be a football player," said Jared, Cindi's brother, who was also coming to camp. Jared's got red hair, like Cindi. He's cute and very sweet. The Pinecones used to tease me that Jared had a crush on me. I don't think so.

"Hey, look who's here," said Jodi. "I wonder why *he* decided to come."

I looked up and saw Heidi and Chris moving through the crowd.

"Hey, Darlene," whispered Cindi. "Don't chew on your lip. You're supposed to smile."

Chris looked terrific. His dark hair was now cut short, shaved in the back, with a flattop in front. He looked taller, and his eyes were still deep blue, so different from Heidi's almost black eyes that you would never guess that Chris and Heidi were brother and sister. But seeing him again made me nervous.

He was grinning. I stopped chewing on my lip and smiled. I was worried that it was a stupid smile.

"Hi, Darlene," he said.

"I like your hair," said Cindi.

"Thanks," said Chris. "This is quite a crowd. I didn't expect so many kids."

"Hi, Chris," said Becky, jabbing an elbow in my side as she pushed me away. "I'm so glad you're here. I'm an old camper. I'll show you the ropes."

"I'll bet," muttered Jodi in my ear. "Don't let her get near Chris."

"He's not exactly my property," I whispered back.

Just then a huge man dressed in neon-green shorts and a yellow sweatshirt saw my dad and gave him a big bear hug. He was almost able to lift Dad off the ground, and Dad weighs nearly two hundred sixty pounds. I'm used to seeing big men, teammates of my dad, but this guy's thighs looked like tree trunks.

"That's got to be Sweet Willie," said Chris. "I remember when he was a player."

"That's him," said the boy talking to Jared. "He's awesome."

"Hi, I'm Chris Ferguson," said Chris to the boy. I forgot how friendly Chris was. Heidi was shy and almost never made the first move. But not Chris.

"Michael Buster," said the boy.

"Buster-Buster, is what we call him," said Becky.

"I decided I hate that name," said Michael.

"Then I'll call you Michael," I said. He looked at me curiously. There weren't many black kids around, and I knew he was guessing that I *had* to be Big Beef's daughter.

"You've got to be a football player," said Chris to Michael.

"Yeah, I can't wait to take coaching from Big Beef," said Michael. "He's my hero."

Jodi giggled. I was feeling a little uncomfortable. This was my nightmare of what this camp would be like: a bunch of jocks all hero worshiping my dad.

"What's your sport?" asked Michael.

"I'm a freestyle skier," said Chris. "But I've trained with these kids at their gym. They're gymnasts."

"Oh, yeah?" said Michael, looking at me. "How good?"

I could tell that I was definitely not going to

like this guy. Luckily before I had to answer his question we were interrupted.

"Buster! Becky!" shrieked a high voice. "You're back!" A tall girl with long tanned legs came up to us. The girl had auburn hair and a really beautiful body. She smiled at Chris. She was exactly his height.

"Hi, you're new," she said, smiling at Chris. "I'm Chelsea. You have any questions about camp, you just ask me." She totally ignored the fact that the six of us Pinecones were also new and standing right next to Chris. It was very clear that she was only interested in talking to him.

"Chelsea," said Becky, "Chris is my special friend."

Cindi started snorting behind me. "You'd better step up and tell those two that Chris and you are 'special friends' before they split him up between them."

"We aren't exactly a couple," I whispered to Cindi.

Somehow Chelsea managed to move Chris away from us and introduced him around to some of the other campers.

"Chelsea is incredibly fast," said Becky.

"I can tell," said Jodi, poking me in the elbow.

"I mean at track and field. That's her sport," said Becky. "Chelsea runs the four forty, and she's already one of the nationally ranked high school athletes, and she's just a freshman."

"She certainly seems to know the ropes," said Cindi.

"Knock it off," I said. "First judgments can be wrong."

Suddenly a whistle blew. Sweet Willie raised his hand. "Campers, new and old, I'm so glad to see you. I know you all have a lot to talk about, but it's time to get on the buses. It's a six-hour trip through the mountains to Woody Creek."

Lauren groaned beside me. I had forgotten how easily Lauren gets carsick.

"Let's get on the bus."

We lined up. Behind me, I could hear Michael whisper to Chris; "Tell me which one's Big Beef's daughter."

I got on the bus and scrunched down in my seat.

"I just knew it was going to be like this," I whispered to Lauren who sat next to me. Cindi and Heidi were behind us. Cindi was draped over the back of my seat and she overheard me.

"You're overreacting," said Cindi. "I don't think your dad is going to be the problem. It'll be hanging on to Chris that will be the challenge."

"Oh, please," I begged. "Chris and I are just friends."

Cindi snorted again. "Well, you'd better not let

Becky hear you say that. She's been wanting a chance to make a play for Chris ever since she met him."

"Well, I'm not going to get in a cat fight with her over him," I said. "Don't worry."

"I just want you to fight for what's yours."

"He's not mine," I insisted. I watched Becky and Chelsea chat up Chris. He seemed to be soaking up all the attention. He didn't look like he minded it *at all*.

Lauren Loses
Her Muffins

Chris and Michael Buster sat in the seats opposite us. Chelsea and Becky were in front of them, both of them twisted around so that they could talk to Chris.

"Did you tell Chris about the commando raids?" Chelsea asked.

"Without a doubt, it's the most fun game in the whole world," said Becky.

"We wait and wait all summer for muffin day," said Michael to Cindi and me.

"What kind of muffins?" asked Lauren. "I love muffins."

Chelsea and Becky started laughing as if Lauren had said the funniest thing in the world.

"Hey, everybody!" shouted Chelsea. "This new kid here loves muffins."

The whole bus laughed.

Lauren turned to me. "Do you have the feeling that everybody's speaking a foreign language?"

"Definitely," I admitted.

"Muffin day," repeated Becky to Chris, as if she wanted to be sure that he wasn't left out. "It's how we find out whether we're commandos or homeguards."

"Oh," said Jodi. "See, Lauren? Now it's perfectly clear."

I giggled.

"It's actually the most important day of the whole summer," said Chelsea sternly, as if I had just suggested burning the flag.

"Muffin day," I said. "The most important day of the year. Blueberry or bran?"

Becky gave me a disgusted look. "There is a piece of paper baked inside each muffin that tells you what team you're on."

"A secret code," said Lauren.

Becky glared at her. Obviously commando raid day was nothing to joke about.

"It's all random," said Chelsea. "The piece of paper in each muffin seals your fate. The game only lasts one day, but it's the best day of the summer."

"Gee, I've always wanted to be a commando," said Jodi.

"It's fun to be a homeguard, too," said Michael, seriously. "You're armed with a squirt gun with red dye in it."

"The commandos have talc bombs," said Chelsea.

"Talc bombs?" Chris asked. He was sounding interested.

"Paper bags filled with talcum powder," explained Becky. "We spend most of the summer making them and filling garbage bags with talc bombs and hiding them around the camp."

"I don't get it," said Heidi. "Does any of this make sense to you?" She leaned forward in her seat.

I shook my head. "It seems to fascinate your brother."

Heidi rolled her eyes. "I think Becky and Chelsea are just fascinated with *him*. Becky's sure decided to make a play for him. You'd better be careful."

"Heidi," I whispered, "I told Cindi, your brother doesn't belong to me."

"Don't you care about him?" asked Heidi.

I didn't answer. Michael Buster was listening to us. I didn't want the whole camp gossiping about me and Chris on the first day.

"Shh," I warned Heidi.

Michael got up and perched on my seat. "You guys will love commando day," he said. "If you get hit, you get striped. Five stripes and you're out, like basketball. It sounds complicated, but as soon as we start playing, it becomes clear."

"Am I stupid or something?" whispered Lauren to me. "Or does this sound like the silliest game in the world?"

"It's certainly got the most complicated rules," I said.

"You don't even know about the supersecret fort," said Becky. "It's the only thing that gives the homeguards a chance. They can move it around, and it's outlined in green and brown string so it's hard to find."

Lauren was beginning to turn a little pale.

"What's the matter with your friend?" asked Chelsea. "Doesn't she like war games?"

"I've never played a war game," said Lauren. "Does this road ever straighten out?" We were climbing up into the mountains, and the road was one continuous switchback. I could feel my ears pop. The bus shifted gears as we turned up another switchback. There was snow on some of the higher peaks, even though it was the first week of July.

"Well, at least it's going to be beautiful," I said to Lauren. I had been in this part of the Rockies, near Aspen, only in the wintertime when we had come skiing with Cindi.

"Hey, Cindi, is this beginning to look familiar?" I asked her.

"It looks totally different in the summer with the trees," said Cindi. "I never imagined it could look so green. Just don't let me turn an ankle hiking."

"I should hope not," said Heidi. "I brought stiff hiking boots." Heidi is always worried about hurting herself. I don't blame her. If I get hurt, a couple of months off isn't going to make the difference between making the Olympics or not. But Heidi can't afford another setback. She already lost several months because of anorexia.

"I broke a leg skiing," said Cindi. "That's the last time I've been around here."

Suddenly Chelsea pointed at Lauren. "Hey, does she always turn that color green?"

I looked at Lauren. "Are you okay?" I asked her.

Lauren had her hand over her mouth. She shook her head no. I could tell she was going to be sick at any moment.

I got up and ran to the front of the bus where Dad was sitting with Sweet Willie.

"Dad," I said, "I think Lauren's going to be sick."

"Oh, no," groaned Dad. He had been on car

trips with Lauren. "Who's Lauren?" asked Sweet Willie.

"She's one of my daughter's teammates," said Dad. "She's a terrific girl. I just wished she had remembered to sit up front."

Sweet Willie got up and pushed past me to the back of the bus. I went after him, worried that maybe he was going to get mad at Lauren for being sick. It wasn't her fault, but from the sound of the commando raids, this camp was run like a Marine boot camp. Maybe new recruits weren't supposed to get sick.

Sweet Willie was leaning over Lauren. "Do you want to come up front?" he asked her kindly.

Lauren shook her head. She was scrunched down in her seat, and she looked absolutely miserable.

Sweet Willie didn't waste any time. "Driver, stop the bus as soon as you find a place that's safe," he shouted. "Stop at the next turnout."

The bus rumbled to the side of the road. "Come on, honey," Sweet Willie said to Lauren. The kids on either side of the aisle ducked as Lauren lurched past them. She threw up as soon as she hit the first step of the bus.

"Oh, yuck. That's disgusting!" said Chelsea.

"She couldn't help herself," said Chris. Sweet Willie held Lauren's head while she threw up again.

"Maybe she couldn't take the idea of commando raids," said Michael.

"Yeah, she lost her muffins, just hearing about them," joked Becky.

"Does she always get sick?" Chelsea asked.

"She's got a delicate stomach," said Becky, somehow making it sound as if Lauren was a little hothouse flower who couldn't be taken anywhere.

Lauren got back on the bus. Sweet Willie had given her a towelette. She sat down.

"Sorry, everybody," she said. She looked horribly embarrassed.

"P.U.," said Michael and held his nose.

The bus started to roll again.

"Are you okay?" I asked Lauren.

"Oh, great," she said sarcastically. "Sweet Willie told me it's another two hours to the camp. I know I'll be sick again, and on top of that, I've got to hear more about these stupid commando raids. I'll never stop heaving."

"Yes, you will," I said optimistically, opening our window as wide as it could go.

Becky and Chelsea were both chattering away to Chris, and he was drinking in every detail they told him about the commando raids.

I glared at them. Somehow I didn't think commando raid day was going to be all that great.

A Course in Gossip

The camp was on a plateau at 10,000 feet where a glacier had come through and flattened a few acres among the high mountains. Wildflowers grew everywhere, and the camp was dotted with huge blue spruce trees that gave us shade from the sun.

Mom and Dad stayed in the Main House next to the mess hall. All the buildings were made out of huge logs. The girls' bunks were on one side of the Main House, and the boys' camp on the other with the football field in the back. There was a river that ran through the camp and a trout pond up behind the main house.

The gym really was a tent, but it was incredibly

beautiful, placed on the top of a knoll overlooking the whole camp. It had been designed by the same company that had built the tent for the Aspen Music Festival. It had no inside tent poles, so when we were on the parallel bars we could really soar without being in any danger of knocking the whole thing down. It looked like a sailing ship plunked down in a meadow of wildflowers. The floor had the familiar blue mats, and all the apparatus was the same, but the tent flaps were left open to the air. When I hung upside down from the high bar, I could sometimes see streaks of snow on the tops of the mountains. Our coach was Maureen. She was very nice, but mostly she taught gym in an elementary school. She just didn't know enough gymnastics to really teach us that much. So we worked out by ourselves, following the routines that Patrick had taught us. Dad says that if he comes back next year, he'll see about getting Patrick a job as coach. The camp really specializes in football and track and field.

Gymnastics were scheduled in the morning while the air was still cool. It was fun because in the first few days we discovered that we Pinecones were much better than most of the other campers. Usually I'm always comparing myself to somebody better than me, like Heidi or Becky.

But here at camp, I was one of the best, and I liked it that way.

Heidi, of course, was outstanding. She ended up coaching. To everyone's surprise, including her own, Heidi turned out to be terrific with the beginners, kids seven and eight years old. She was patient with them, something she never is with herself.

Cindi and I watched Heidi as she had six little girls lined up on the beam. They looked like tiny blue jays on a telephone wire.

"They're sitting ducks for talc bombs," said Becky, toweling herself off. Becky did not help with the little kids much. She did her routines and stayed in shape, but that was about it.

"Can't you think of anything except that game?" I asked her.

"Yeah," said Becky. "How cute Chris looks on the trampoline." She looked over at Chris. Then she giggled. "Actually he looks cute doing anything. We're playing tennis later. I asked him, and he said yes. In fact, I'd better hurry. It's kind of a date." Becky rushed out of the tent.

"I think you should talc her," said Cindi.

"She doesn't bother me," I lied.

"Well, she should," said Cindi.

"Darlene has been slow in making talc bombs," teased Lauren.

It was true. We had been at camp less than three days, and the rest of the Pinecones had gotten into making talc bombs. The bombs were just little paper bags that you had to fill with talcum powder and tie with a plastic tie.

The talc was stored in the arts-and-crafts tent, and campers were allowed to go in there during their free periods and make bombs. It was everybody's favorite activity, except mine. Our bunk now has two huge green trash bags filled with finished talc bombs. I had made only three of the bombs.

Cindi put her arm around me. "Come on, Darlene," she said. "We've got a free period. Let's go make you some talc bombs."

"I guess I can't put it off forever," I said. I didn't want to play tennis and have to watch Becky and Chris.

"Where are you going now?" asked Heidi, letting the little kids off the beam.

"To shower and then to make talc bombs," I said.

"Whooee!" said Heidi. "I'll go, too."

"Me, too," said Ti An.

After our showers, we went over to the arts-and-crafts tent. Becky's friend Chelsea was there, along with a boy named Steven who was Michael Buster's best friend. As soon as we walked in they started whispering together.

I sat down at one of the benches and got a couple of paper bags.

"Oh, shoot," I said. Talcum powder spilled all over my best pair of jeans. It is not the easiest job in the world to transfer loose talcum powder from a metal container to a little paper bag. "I shouldn't have bothered to shower."

The whole arts-and-crafts tent looked like something out of *The Revenge of the Sugar Doughnuts.* Powder was in the air and in every corner.

"I really want at least one of us Pinecones to be on the winning team," said Lauren, fiercely. Her face was a picture of complete concentration as she twisted the tie around the neck of the paper bag.

Lauren was the last person I expected to get into the commando game. She had been teased because she had ended up throwing up five times on our way to camp. She had immediately and methodically begun making bombs. I think she and Ti An were about even for making the most bombs in our bunk.

"Come on, Darlene," urged Cindi. "This is no time to worry about getting dirty."

"The reason Darlene doesn't like making bombs is that she doesn't like getting her clothes messy," said Chelsea to Steven.

"You don't know me," I said.

"Well, I've heard how much you like clothes," said Chelsea. She giggled to Steven as if she had just said something witty.

"Yeah, almost as much as she likes Chris," said Steven, with a giggle.

"Yeah, she wants to keep neat and clean for her boyfriend," teased Chelsea.

This drove me crazy. Kids whom I didn't even know were gossiping about me.

"I think Chris likes Becky more than Darlene, anyhow," said Chelsea.

I stood up and brushed the talcum powder off me. "Would you kids mind your own beeswax?"

"Oh, look," said Chelsea, pointing down toward the tennis courts. "There go Becky and Chris. They do look cute together,"

I looked out the flap. Becky and Chris *were* walking toward the tennis courts together.

It made me mad. I shoved too much talc into the paper bag, and it ripped and I got more talcum powder all over me. Chelsea and Steven laughed.

"I hate this stupid game," I muttered. "I probably won't ever get to throw a talc bomb."

"It's a proven fact that more talc bombs end up being lost and never used than ever get thrown," said Lauren.

"That's why it's a good thing that talc is a natural mineral," said Ti An. "And the paper bags are biodegradable. We're not hurting the environment."

"Great," I said sarcastically. "An evironmentally correct war game."

"The only ones who don't like this game are wimps who are afraid of competition," said Chelsea.

"Darlene is *not* a wimp," said Lauren. Somehow I wish she hadn't said that. It made me sound like such a dork.

Chelsea and Steven laughed. They stuffed their bombs into their knapsacks. "Now we've got to figure out a place to hide them," said Chelsea. "Where no wimps can find them."

They left. I made another bomb, muttering to myself the whole time.

"Darlene," said Cindi. "I just don't see why you're down on this game. I think it's going to be loads of fun."

Lauren had a topographical map of the area from the National Forest Service and was making little *x*'s on it.

"What are you doing?" I asked.

"I'm marking where I've hidden my talc bombs," said Lauren.

"You kids have got commando raid on the brain," I said.

"Maybe Chelsea had a point," said Heidi.

"Maybe you are afraid of a little competition."

"What does that mean?" I asked.

"You don't like fighting for Chris," said Heidi. "That's your problem."

"It wouldn't hurt if you minded your own business, too," I said a little more sharply than I expected.

"My brother *is* my business," said Heidi. "Do you think I like Becky hanging all over him?"

"Besides," said Jodi, "there's the honor of the Pinecones to consider. We never let Becky take something that is ours."

"Look," I said, getting angry, "in the first place, Chris does not belong to the Pinecones. He is not our property. He doesn't even belong to you, Heidi."

"I know that," she said. "But I though you liked my brother. If you did, you wouldn't just let Becky have him."

"I am not letting her 'have' him. I can't help it if he's playing tennis with Becky."

"We want you to tell Becky to get lost," said Cindi.

"Oh, right, and have the whole camp gossiping about us. Thanks a million."

"The whole camp's gossiping anyhow," said Cindi. "I heard Michael Buster tell Jared that Becky told him that she and Chris were going together. That made Jared happy because — "

"Oh, give me a break," I said. "We didn't come up to the Rocky Mountains to take a course in gossip."

"Actually," teased Jodi, "I think gossip is a great game. Almost as much fun as commando raids."

Down and Dirty

We were just starting our second week of camp. We were working out in the tent. I was helping Heidi spot the little kids on the uneven bars. They were so tiny I had to lift them up to reach the lower bar. Naturally Becky was working out by herself on the beam.

Chris came over. He had been working out on the trampoline. He had a towel around his neck. He looked good.

"Need any help?" he asked.

I shook my head. "Naw, I just get them started. Your sister does all the work."

I gave my little charge a pat on the back and stepped aside. Heidi helped the kid through her routine.

"It's amazing, isn't it?" he said. "Heidi gets such a kick out of those little kids."

"She's good with them," I said.

"So are you," said Chris.

I bit my lip. Chris and I hadn't been talking much the first week of camp. It seemed that every time we were alone, Becky always found us. The Pinecones weren't really helping. They kept urging me to "fight for Chris," which I found totally humiliating.

"Say," said Chris. "I'm going riding right after my workout. Do you want to come?"

I smiled, feeling more like grinning. It was the first time Chris had asked me to do anything with him alone. Maybe I wouldn't have to fight for him, after all.

"Sure," I said.

"Becky said she'd show Heidi and me some great trails that I haven't seen before."

"Super," I said. Chris didn't catch the sarcasm in my voice. I did not want Becky along on any ride with Chris, and I was sure that Becky would feel the exact same way about me coming along. On the other hand, it would really put her nose out of joint if I went, and I couldn't pass up a chance to put that stuck-up nose out of joint.

"It'll be fun," I said to Chris.

Heidi finished her session with the little kids. She came up to us, smiling. The mountain air

had really relaxed her. The other Pinecones finished their workouts, too.

"Ready to go horseback riding?" Chris asked
Heidi. She shook her head. "Naw, I decided to
go white-water rafting with Jodi, Cindi, and Ti
An instead. Our counselor is going to take us.
Horseback riding is too dangerous."

I laughed at Heidi. She has incredible rules for
herself about what is or is not dangerous. She
is famous for her daredevil release moves from
the high bar. I've watched her soar about six feet
over the bar, something that only the men used
to do, and catch the bar at the last millisecond.
Heidi doesn't consider that dangerous. Any other
sport where she might hurt herself, however, is
considered too risky. Yet, here she was going
white-water rafting.

"Darlene, do you still want to come riding with
me?" Chris asked. "Or would you rather go
white-water rafting?"

"Riding!" Cindi answered for me.

I shook my head. "Cindi!" I whispered. She just
giggled. Heidi winked at me.

"I don't think Becky would want me along," I
said to Chris.

"All the more reason why you *should* go," said
Heidi, right in front of her brother. It was *so*
embarrassing.

Chris didn't look embarrassed at all. "It'll be

okay with Becky," he said confidently. "She wants to show me some good places to hide bombs. We promised each other that if we were on opposite teams we wouldn't divulge the secret. I'm sure Becky will trust Darlene, too."

"Oh, sure she will," I said, trying not to guffaw.

Becky saw us talking together and jumped off the beam in the middle of her routine.

"Hi, Chris," she said, ignoring the rest of us. "I'll be ready for our horseback ride soon."

"Hi," said Chris. "I asked Darlene to come riding with us."

Becky glared at me. "Chris is a good rider, and so am I. Are you sure you can keep up?"

"Yes!" Cindi answered for me. She seemed to have decided that I couldn't take care of myself.

Becky whispered something in Chris's ear. I hate people who tell secrets in front of me. It always makes me feel they're whispering about me, and in Becky's case, I was positive that I was right.

Chris shrugged. He smiled a little sheepishly at me. "Becky's a little upset," he said.

"I am not," protested Becky. I knew she was waiting for me to say that I wouldn't go riding. I was *not* going to give her the satisfaction.

"What's the matter, Becky?" I asked. "Don't you want company?"

"It's not that," said Becky. "I'm just worried

that too many people will know where we've hidden our bombs."

"Don't worry," I said. "I couldn't care less about the stupid commando raids."

Becky laughed at me. "That's just because you've never played the game."

"Right," teased Cindi. "It's time to get down and dirty, Darlene."

I laughed. I knew Cindi wasn't talking about the commando raids. Well, if it was a fight Becky wanted, I wasn't going to back off.

8

Hard to Control

Down at the stable, I asked for Lady Guinevere.

"That old nag," said Becky. "I want Sir Lancelot."

"Lady G is not an old nag," I protested. She was my favorite horse. She was a chestnut mare with white markings. Nearly fourteen years old, she still had a spring in her trot and an incredibly comfortable canter.

"I'll take Centerfold," said Chris. Centerfold was a three-year-old mare who was Lady G's filly.

"I think that's a tacky name for a horse," I said.

"Well, you've got to admit she's pretty," said Chris, "and she's got good form."

"She was supposed to be a champion show horse, but she just doesn't like to jump," said

Becky. "At least she's got spirit, not like Lady G."

"Lady G has plenty of spirit," I protested.

"I don't want to jump, either," said Chris, clearly wanting to change the subject. He patted Centerfold on the neck. I wished I knew what Chris felt. Did he really like Becky more than me?

Becky mounted Sir Lancelot, who's a big horse, and who I think has kind of a nasty disposition. Maybe that's why Becky liked him. "I've been riding since I was four years old," boasted Becky. "All native born Coloradans know how to ride. You're not native born, are you, Darlene?"

"No," I said. "I was born in Georgia." I mounted up. I learned to ride on my great-grandmother GeeGee's farm in Georgia. GeeGee believed that it was best to learn bareback, so I had really learned the feel of a horse. I might not be a show-off like Becky, but I knew my way around horses.

We headed down the trail, following the path by the river, our talc bombs in our knapsacks. Becky's horse shook his head and moved in a circle. She was holding the reins too tightly. "He's got so much spirit. He's hard to control," Becky bragged. She was the kind of rider who had to show the horse immediately that *she* was the boss.

"Try loosening the reins a little," I said. "You're dragging the bit against the tender part of his mouth."

"You don't know this horse," said Becky. "He's not like your horse." Sir Lancelot was obviously getting very annoyed. He did a tiny buck, throwing his back legs into the air and shaking his head again.

"See? He tried to throw me," said Becky.

"He didn't try to throw you. He's just trying to get the bit to stop hurting him," I argued. I hated riders like Becky. Everything was always the horse's fault, never their fault.

"I think I know what I'm doing," argued Becky. "I rode this horse all last summer. You weren't even here."

"Right," I muttered. Chris trotted up beside me. "You look good on Lady G," he said. "You two look like you were made for each other."

"Lady G is the horse they give to all the little kids," said Becky. "She's so gentle nothing will spook her."

"There's nothing wrong with being gentle," I said.

"I think we should canter," said Becky. Becky dug her heels in front of the cinch into the thick muscle of Sir Lancelot's rib cage. Naturally he didn't feel a thing.

I squeezed my legs and kicked backward. Lady G responded immediately. We sprinted ahead of Becky. Lady G had long legs, and her slow canter covered a lot of ground. I opened up space between Becky and me. We reached a high ridge above the camp. I could see the other Pinecones putting their raft into the river. I looked over my shoulder. Chris had gotten Centerfold into a nice canter, but all Sir Lancelot would do was a fast trot. Becky bounced up and down, waving her reins in the air and throwing them from side to side, trying to force Sir Lancelot into a canter. She wasn't having any luck.

I slowed Lady G down to a trot and then a walk. Chris's face was flushed.

"That was fun," he said. "Why did you stop?"

"Becky was having trouble," I said. Becky bounced up to us. "Next time we canter, if you keep Sir Lancelot right behind me, he'll follow Lady G's lead," I said. "Horses are herd animals. They like to do what all the others are doing."

"Kind of like Pinecones," muttered Becky.

"Are you okay?" Chris asked her. "I'm sorry you didn't get to canter. It was fun."

"Darlene is totally wrong," said Becky. "I wasn't cantering because I didn't want to." Becky stopped near an aspen tree and tore off a small branch to use as a crop.

"Don't do that," I said. "Sweet Willie told me that aspen trees can't grow the branch back. They're not like other trees. Their bark is like our skin. If you cut it, it bleeds, and it can kill the tree. If you take off a branch, it's like cutting off a finger."

"I think I know a little bit more about these woods than you do," said Becky. "I've heard of bleeding-heart liberals, but this is the first time I've heard of bleeding-heart aspens, right, Chris?"

"I didn't know that about aspen trees," said Chris.

"I think Darlene's making it up," said Becky, smiling at him. "I've noticed all the Pinecones have lively imaginations. Besides," she whispered loudly enough for me to hear, "Darlene will do anything to make me look bad."

"That's not true," I protested. We continued through a pine forest, the big spruces giving plenty of shade from the sun. It was a beautiful trail, and one that I had never been on before. I decided to try to enjoy myself, despite Becky.

We hadn't gone more than a hundred yards when Sir Lancelot spotted a white mulberry bush that must have looked particularly tasty to him. He stopped and started eating.

"Don't let him eat," I said without thinking. Eating on the trail is the worst habit for saddle horses to get into. If one rider lets a horse eat, it will always assume that it's okay. "Pull up his head," I said.

Becky glared at me. "It so happens that I asked him to find this particular bush," she said.

Chris started to snicker. "Becky, come off it. Pull up his head, and let's keep going."

"No," insisted Becky. "This is the bush where I wanted to hide my talc bombs."

Becky got off her horse. Chris got off, too, and helped Becky dig a hole to bury her talc bombs.

"Darlene, do you want to bury yours here, too?" asked Chris. I looked around. I really didn't want anything of mine connected with Becky, even my stupid talc bombs.

Lady Guinevere's ears twitched. I followed her eyes. She had spotted a gooseberry bush. It was full of berries. I slid off the saddle and walked Lady G over. I hooked the lead line over a spruce tree's branch and tied it.

Then I shoved my talc bombs under the bush. It didn't seem worth the bother to bury them. I started eating the berries. I couldn't believe how tart they tasted.

Suddenly I heard a rustle behind me. I jumped, thinking it could be a bear. Bears love gooseberries, too.

"Snack time," said a voice.

I giggled. "I guess you aren't a bear," I said to Chris.

He picked a berry. "Now, this is more fun than commando fights." He picked another and held it out for me to eat. It was a particularly good one.

We heard footsteps coming closer. I knew it must be Becky. I decided I might as well be civilized. "Becky, we're over here, in the gooseberry patch," I said.

"Oh, good," said Becky.

I heard leaves rustle and then a loud swat. I heard a whinny and then another swat and then the sound of hooves scrambling through the underbrush.

I took off toward the tree where I had tethered Lady G.

Becky was standing with her hands on her hips. "I can't believe you didn't know enough to tie up your horse," she said. "I tried to stop her, but she ran away."

Becky looked at Chris as if to say what a dolt I was. I ran down the trail. Sometimes a horse will be spooked and just run a little bit away and then stop. But I could see Lady G's rump way in the distance. I knew horses, and I knew where she was going. She was going straight home to the stables.

I kicked at a loose stone. I knew I had tied her up.

I went to the spruce tree. There were no scratch marks on the branch as if the horse had forced the reins off. I saw a loose aspen branch under the tree. I picked it up. It was freshly snapped off.

I looked at Becky who had mounted her horse. She was no longer carrying a crop.

"Why don't you start walking toward camp," said Becky, "and Chris and I will go look for Lady Guinevere?"

"Thanks," I said sarcastically.

Chris looked down at me from Centerfold. "You don't have to walk home. If I go slowly, Centerfold can carry both our weight."

"I was planning on getting in a good canter on the way back," said Becky.

Chris just looked at her. "I'm not leaving Darlene to walk home by herself."

"I'm not scared of bears," I joked.

Chris held a hand out. I grabbed it and swung up onto the saddle behind him. I had to put my hands around his waist for balance. Being that close felt good, and I knew it annoyed the dickens out of Becky. I liked that.

9

Not a Pretty Sight

When we got back to the stable, there was Lady Guinevere happily munching on her hay.

Marta, the riding counselor, looked furious. "I was about to send a posse after you. I was worried when Lady G came back without a rider."

"We stopped to eat some berries, and she got loose," I said. I may be many things, but I'm not a tattletale.

Chris gave me a strange look. Becky dismounted and rubbed the dust off her jodhpurs. "It ruined our ride," she whined.

"It wasn't Darlene's fault that Lady G got loose," said Chris.

Becky looked guilty. For a moment, I thought

she was going to yell at Chris. Then she got control of herself and smiled.

"Oh, I know," she said. "It was just an accident."

"Some accident," I muttered to myself.

"What exactly do you mean?" demanded Becky. She stood with her feet wide apart, challenging me. I wasn't planning on accusing her, but she was just daring me to say something. I couldn't resist a dare.

"I *know* exactly what happened out there on the trail," I said. I took Lady G's saddle off.

"I hate whiners," said Chris. Both Becky and I stopped in our tracks. I was pretty sure he didn't mean me. I hadn't been whining. On the other hand, what if he thought I had deliberately let Lady G go so that I would get to ride double with him? It would be so humiliating if he thought that. I couldn't stand it.

I took Lady G's lead rope and started to walk her in circles, giving us both a chance to cool down.

"I'm going to the showers," said Becky.

Chris watched her go. I still couldn't tell what he was thinking. "I'll see you later," he said to me. He didn't sound overly friendly.

After Lady G was good and cool, I led her to the stall and went back to my bunk.

The kids who had gone white-water rafting

were already there when I got back. I told them what had happened.

"You should have come white-water rafting with us," said Lauren. "It was awesome. We went over some rapids that were incredible."

"And guess who didn't get seasick?" said Ti An.

Lauren pointed a finger at herself proudly. "I was too busy paddling," said Lauren. "I think that's the secret. If I had driven the bus, I wouldn't have gotten carsick."

"Watch out, world, when Lauren gets her driver's license!" said Cindi.

Becky came into the bunk, fresh from the showers. She had a clean bandanna around her neck. Becky must have a million of them. She purposely didn't speak to me, as she lay down and put her Walkman on.

"Becky, I guess your horseback ride with Chris wasn't quite what you expected," said Heidi.

Becky ignored her.

"Leave her alone," I said. "It's been a long day."

"I wish they'd have the commando game tomorrow," said Ashley. "I'm getting tired of waiting."

Just then there was a knock on the door to our cabin. Dad stuck his head in.

"Hi, girls," he said. "Is it okay if I come in? I've got presents for you."

"You're going to spill the beans on when commando day is going to be!" said Jodi eagerly. "That's the best present you could give us."

"Sorry," said Dad. "My lips are sealed on that one." He took out a green garbage bag from behind his back.

"Duck!" yelled Cindi. "It could be talc bombs. Maybe this is the way commando raids start."

"It starts with muffins, dummy," said Ashley. "Even you have to know that." Sometimes Ashley did sound like a perfect Becky imitation.

"It's picture day," said Dad. He pulled out a red T-shirt with my name written in big black letters across the front. He turned the shirt around. It read *Sweet Willie's Sports Camp* with an outline of mountains.

It was a true red, and I loved the color. "Is mine the only one that has a name on it?" I asked tentatively.

Dad reached into the bag and started tossing the shirts at different girls. Our names were on each one. Becky pulled her earphones off. She looked interested.

"Say," said Becky, admiring her shirt, "this is the first year that we've had our names on our T-shirts."

"That was my idea," said Dad proudly. "I figured football players and basketball players have their names on their shirts — why not campers?

It'll make it easier for your parents to see you in the camp photographs."

"Dad," I complained. "You should have given us warning about picture day. I just came back from a horseback ride."

"And she wants to look pretty for Chris," teased Cindi.

Becky glared at her.

"Where do you take the pictures?" I asked. "Give us a few minutes to get ready. Can we have ours taken in front of the gymnastics tent?"

"Great idea," agreed Dad. "I'll tell the photographer to meet you up there."

"Traditionally we alway have it taken in front of the goal posts on the football field," complained Becky.

"Some traditions are meant to be changed," said Dad. "Put on your T-shirts and meet us up there."

We put on the T-shirts. I liked mine because it was big and covered my butt. I love oversize T-shirts.

"Aren't you going to complain that yours doesn't fit you right?" said Becky nastily.

"I like it like this," I said. Becky had been given an extra-large, too. I tied the bottom into a knot at my waist. Becky tied hers into a knot, too.

Cindi giggled and did the same with her T-shirt. Her red hair sprang out in all directions.

"Redheads shouldn't wear red," said Becky.

"Not true," I said, "Cindi looks great in red."

"Besides," said Ashley, "look, you can turn them inside out. Then it's black with our names in red."

"It means that commando day is near," said Becky. "Because on commando day, you wear red if you're a commando and black if you're a homeguard."

"I want to be a commando," said Jodi, "definitely."

"You don't get a choice," said Becky. "You have to take whatever muffin is on your plate. The counselors watch us like hawks to make sure nobody switches."

"I bet she sneaks some way to be on Chris's team," whispered Cindi.

"Don't worry about it," I said. I looked at myself in the little mirror I kept on the shelf by my bed. "Come on, let's go."

We went out into the sunshine and up to the gymnastics tent.

The photographer had set up in front of the tent. "Let's get a picture of you all up on the beam together," he said. "Uh, let's see, why don't we have the blonde next to Big Beef's daughter."

Jodi and Becky looked at each other. "We're both blonde," said Jodi. "Which one of us do you want?"

"I was talking to the one with the red bandanna," said the photographer. Becky stood next to me.

I giggled. "What's so funny?" Becky snapped at me, sure that I was making fun of her.

"It's not you," I said. "Stop being so sensitive."

Becky just glared at me.

The photographer interrupted. "Excuse me, would the blonde in the bandanna smile. And the little Asian girl, give me a big smile, move a little in front of the girl with short hair."

I couldn't take it anymore. I started laughing so hard, I couldn't stop.

The photographer smiled at me. "Uh . . . I want this to look informal, but would the girl who's laughing keep it down a little? I just want a big smile, not a big laugh."

"It's Darlene," I said to the photographer, pointing to the name on my T-shirt. "All you have to do is look at our T-shirts to tell who we are."

The photographer looked up from his camera. He grinned. "I guess that does make me look a little stupid."

"Don't worry," said Becky. "Darlene specializes in making people look stupid."

"I do not," I said, furious that Becky would think that of me.

"Yes, you do," snapped Becky. "Look what you did on the horseback ride."

"*You* were the one . . ." I sputtered.

"Okay, girls," interrupted the photographer. "Remember, this is a sports camp. Look athletic."

I flexed my biceps and made a fist with my right hand and shook it at Becky. I was just kidding around, but I must have surprised Becky. Maybe she thought I was really going to hit her although I never would. She fell off the beam. And that's when the photographer snapped our picture. It was not a pretty sight.

The Pinecones all started laughing and posing as if we were weight lifters. Becky glared up at us, but the Pinecones couldn't stop laughing. Even Ashley was giggling. The Pinecones were happy, but I never really wanted Becky as an enemy. And now she had even more reason to hate me. I didn't like being hated. I wasn't sure that even Chris was worth it.

10

Stars at Noon

Over the next few days, I hardly talked to Chris alone at all. It seemed that every time I saw him, Becky was draped over his shoulder, or else he was in the middle of a crowd, and Becky was right there with him.

I tried to pretend that I didn't notice, but it was hard. The only time I really got to see Chris up close was when he was working out in the tent while we did our gymnastics in the early morning cool before breakfast.

I could see him now out of the corner of my eye while I was spotting for Ti An while she practiced a handspring to a backward somersault. She spun around so fast that I only needed to touch her back for her to make it all the way around.

She finished at the edge of the mat and turned and grinned at me.

"That was great," I said.

"I think it's the altitude," said Ti An. "Tennis balls bounce higher here, and so do we."

"It's not the altitude," Heidi said. "I think it's the *attitude*. Everybody's so relaxed that you're all doing better."

"What about you?" I kidded her. "You're positively loosey-goosey."

"Yeah, unfortunately altitude hasn't changed Becky's attitude," said Cindi. "Look at her."

Becky was lounging around the mats by the trampoline where Chris was working out.

"Poor Chris," said Jodi. "Everywhere he goes, Becky's after him."

"I told you before I don't think Chris really hates the attention," I said.

"Still it should make you mad," said Lauren. "Chris was interested in you first. I still think he likes you best."

I looked over at Becky and Chris. It did make me mad, but I just couldn't afford to give Becky the satisfaction of knowing it did. Besides, it was a little Chris's fault. He could have found ways to brush her off, but he didn't.

"Could we please talk about something else?" I begged.

"Yeah, let's talk about the fact that Michael Buster asked Jodi to teach him how to do a flip."

"Michael Buster? Doing a flip?" I exclaimed. "He'll kill himself."

"I thought I'd start with teaching him in the pool," said Jodi.

"Michael and Jodi . . . Michael and Jodi . . . It has such a pretty sound," teased Lauren.

"Cut it out," protested Jodi. "You're just jealous, 'cause his best friend, Steven, didn't ask you to go white-water rafting."

"Eleven-year-olds," Heidi whispered to me. "I think they do much more gossiping than anything else. If a boy came near one of them, they'd run for the hills."

I laughed. Heidi had a point. I looked at her brother and Becky. Chris saw me staring and waved. I turned away. Ever since our horseback ride, I was absolutely sure he was spending more time with Becky than with me. He must have believed Becky's story that I had let Lady G go. I didn't want him to see that it bothered me, but I was hurt.

We finished our workout and walked out of the tent.

Mom caught me just as I was going toward the mess hall for breakfast.

64

"I like your T-shirt," she said. I was wearing my shirt with the black side out and my name in red letters.

"Hi, Darlene," said a boy I didn't even really know.

"Hi," I said tentatively.

Then another boy I didn't know also said hi. I made a face.

"What's that for?" Mom asked.

"Everybody's saying hello to me, even kids I don't really know. They know my name just because they know I'm Big Beef's daughter," I complained.

Mom started laughing.

"What's so funny?" I asked her.

"Look at your shirt," said Mom. I looked down. There in the big red letters was my name. "That's why they know your name," Mom said.

"I guess the joke's on me," I said. "I'm glad Becky didn't hear me. I made fun of the photographer the other day because he wouldn't use our names even though they were on the front of our shirts."

Mom looked up and saw Becky and Chris walking together. They were in earnest conversation.

"Is Becky giving you problems?" Mom asked.

"Nothing I can't handle," I said to Mom.

"What about Chris?" Mom asked. "Are you still friends?"

I didn't want to talk to Mom about my problems with Chris. I saw the Pinecones hurrying for breakfast.

"Mom, I've got to go," I said.

"Have a good breakfast," said Mom. There was something in her voice that sounded a little funny.

I stopped in my tracks. I looked at Mom. "Do you know something about today being the day for the commando raids?"

"Me?" said Mom. "I have nothing to do with the commando raid affair. Personally, my idea of fun does not include getting squirted with dye or bombarded with talcum powder."

She sounded sincere, but on the other hand she had a kind of weird smile on her face.

I ran off to join the Pinecones. Michael and Jared were with them. "What did your Mom have to say?" asked Lauren.

"Nothing," I said, "but to be on the safe side, I think we'd better take a close look at our muffins today."

Chris and Becky joined us. "Darlene thinks commando day might be today," said Heidi.

"Never," said Becky. "They never have it on a Wednesday. It's against tradition. Darlene doesn't know anything."

"I think they had it on Wednesday once," said Michael.

"No, they didn't," insisted Becky.

Michael shrugged his shoulders. "They did," he whispered to me.

I giggled. I had a feeling that if I said the stars shone at night, she would say they were brighter at noon. If I said that Chris liked her more than he liked me — that's about the only statement in the world Becky and I would agree on. And that was one statement I hoped wasn't true.

It's Not a Game
— It's War!

We sat down at the long wooden tables. Mom and Dad were at the head table with Sweet Willie and his wife. After we'd been served our juice and hot cereal, Sweet Willie rang his fork against his water glass and stood up for the morning announcements.

"Good morning, everybody," he boomed out.

We boomed back, "Good morning!"

"The sun is shining. It looks like a beautiful day. Let's pass the muffins."

There was a bloodcurdling scream that literally shook the mess hall. A hundred kids started stamping their feet and pounding the tops of the tables as they yelled at the tops of their lungs.

"I guess today is it," Chris whispered to me. "I

wonder if we'll be on the same team."

I wished he had said that he *hoped* we'd be on the same team.

The muffins came around the table. The counselors didn't let us choose. They put one on each of our plates. They all looked alike.

"Chris, we've just got to be commandos together," gushed Becky. She broke her muffin open and took out a greasy piece of paper. Her face fell. I thought for a moment she was going to cry. "Homeguard!" she said. "There's got to be a mistake." She made a motion to get another muffin, but a counselor saw her and shook her head.

I broke open my muffin. "Commando," I said.

"Me, too!" shrieked Ti An.

"I'm a homeguard," said Jodi. She sounded disappointed.

"Me, too," said Cindi.

We looked at each other. We had never been on opposite teams before.

Lauren opened her muffin. "I'm a commando, too," she said. She and Cindi kept staring at their pieces of paper. They've been best friends since kindergarten.

"It's only a game," I said. "And it just lasts for one day."

"I'm a commando!" screeched Heidi. She gave me a high five. "Hey, bro, what are you?"

Chris was still fingering his muffin as if he didn't really want to open it.

"Come on, Chris," urged Becky.

Chris broke it open. "Homeguard," he read out loud. Becky let out a whoop of glee. "All right!" she said. "This is going to be one year when the homeguard wins. Besides, squirt guns are so much more fun than talc bombs."

"How did she do that?" Cindi whispered to me.

"It's got to be luck," I whispered back. "The counselors were watching. There's no way she could have switched Chris's muffin."

"I bet," sniffed Cindi.

"No," I said. "I was watching his muffin all the time. Becky didn't touch it."

It was the truth. Maybe Chris and I weren't meant to be on the same team.

Michael Buster came over to our table. "Any commandos over here?" Lauren, Ti An, Ashley, Heidi, and I all raised our hands.

"Come on," said Michael. "We've got only an hour to get organized. Let's go. I'm the captain of this team."

"Don't we get to eat the muffins?" asked Lauren.

Michael just stared at her. "*Everybody* is *always* too excited to eat the muffins," he said disdainfully.

Lauren stuffed a piece of muffin into her

mouth. "How did he get to be captain?" she muttered, her mouth full.

"I have a feeling he appointed himself," I whispered back. We got up from our table.

"Good luck, you guys," I said to Chris, Cindi, and Jodi.

Becky sneered at me. "This is war, Darlene. You don't wish the other side good luck in war."

"It's not war. It's a game," I insisted.

"Not for the next few hours," said Becky. "Chris, we're going to hide the supersecret fort where the commandos will never find it. That trophy is *ours*." Becky put her arm around Chris's neck and started whispering stategy into his ear.

"Hey," said Jodi, "remember? Cindi and I are on your team, too."

Becky looked a little annoyed. Basically Becky didn't like any of the Pinecones, but Jodi was probably her least favorite.

Sweet Willie rang his glass again.

"I just want to go over the rules for everybody. Right after breakfast, everybody puts on his or her T-shirt. Red for commandos. Black for the homeguard. Stick with your teams. Remember it's a game. Don't go off by yourselves, and don't get lost.

"The homeguard will have five forts that are outlined with white string. These forts have already been put into place by the counselors. The commandos will have to find them and bombard them with talc. The supersecret fort is outlined in brown and green string so that it blends in with the ground. This fort can be moved by the homeguard if they think it's about to be discovered. If the commandos can capture this fort, they win automatically.

"If any of you commandos get squirted with red dye, you have to come up here to the mess hall to get striped. It's the same for those homeguards who get talced. Five stripes and you're out of the game. Any questions?"

"Yes," I yelled. "Who invented this game, anyhow?"

"It's the most fun game in the whole world!" yelled all the old campers in unison.

"Let's go," said Michael. "Everybody put on your shirt with the red side out, and we'll meet by the trout pond. We've got to take to the woods."

The commandos filed out of the mess hall. Just as we were about to move out, Jodi came up to me.

"Don't worry," she whispered. "Cindi and I'll try to keep Becky and Chris in separate forts."

"It's not a problem," I insisted, although I couldn't believe Becky's luck. It would have been easier if I just could have blamed Becky's normal deviousness. Now I had to think that maybe fate hadn't meant for Chris and I to be together.

"Jodi!" yelled Becky. "Get back here. You can't fraternize with the enemy!"

"Enemy?" giggled Jodi. "It's Darlene."

"Enemy!" repeated Becky.

"Come on, Jodi," said Chris. "It may be just a game, but don't give away any secrets."

Jodi slunk back to her team.

Chris wouldn't even look at me. Suddenly I wanted to show the two of them that I could play this stupid game as well as they did. I was a commando, and maybe Becky was right. It wasn't just a game. It was war.

12

We Lost That Round

"Okay," yelled Michael, when we had all gath-erd at the trout pond, "we've got to put mud on our faces."

"Isn't it more important that we gather up our talc bombs?" asked Lauren. "I know exactly where I hid mine."

Michael gave her a patronizing look. "I've played this game for years," he said.

He dropped down beside the bank and started to smear mud on his cheeks and forehead and up and down his forearms.

"Come on, Darlene," he said. "You've got to get camouflaged."

I sighed. "Michael, you might not have noticed, but I come already camouflaged."

Lauren giggled.

"Besides," said Ashley, "Darlene doesn't like to get dirty."

"We don't call Ashley 'Becky-in-training' for nothing," muttered Lauren.

"I think too much exposure to Becky at this camp has been bad for her," I said.

"Lauren! Darlene!" snapped Michael in his best major-general voice. "Get down and dirty. You're not a commando unless you get mud on your face."

Ashley tittered. Heidi was seriously applying mud all over herself.

"Okay, okay," said Lauren, patting mud on her face. "It's a proven fact that this is an ancient beauty treatment."

I looked at Lauren. She had mud caked in her short dark hair. "Some beauty treatment," I joked. But I obediently began to smear mud on my face and arms. It actually felt good and cool.

"Now what?" asked Ti An, eagerly.

"Now, we gather our talc bombs," said Michael. "Then we'll split up and look for the forts. They always have one somewhere near the football field. We'll go there first."

Michael had a stash of talc bombs planted right by a cottonwood tree near the river. Another kid had some a little farther down the river by an aspen.

"Where are yours, Darlene?" Michael asked me.

"They're up above, on the plateau. I put them there when I went horseback riding with Becky."

"That's a stupid place to hide them," said Michael. "There are never any forts up there."

"Becky told me that was the best place," I said.

"And you fell for that old trick?" said Michael. "All old campers try to fool the new campers into planting their talc bombs where they'll never use them."

I groaned.

"What's wrong?" asked Ti An.

"Becky," I muttered. "She made me hide my bombs in a place where I can't use them. I wonder what else she did to me."

"Tried to steal your boyfriend," said Lauren.

"He's not my boyfriend," I protested. I scratched at the mud on my face. It felt itchy. If Chris saw me now, he'd never like me anyhow. Maybe Becky was more his type in the first place. "Well, he's on Becky's team," I said. "There's nothing I can do about it."

"That's what you've been saying all summer," said Lauren. "That you have nothing to fight with."

"It's okay," said Ti An. "You can use some of my talc bombs." I laughed. Ti An always took things so literally.

"Thanks," I said. We sneaked through the woods toward the football field.

Suddenly Michael let out a loud, *"Yee-yee-yee . . . o!"* He charged down the hill, toward the football field. I could see the white lines of a homeguard fort. Chris popped up in front of the fort and squirted Michael with a steady stream of red dye. Then he turned and got his sister.

Michael fell backward, pretending to grab his chest. "I'm hit . . . I'm hit," he yelled. "But I won't give up!" Michael pretended to stagger toward the fort.

"Come on, Michael," complained Becky, giving up her hiding place from behind a tree. "You've been hit. You've got to stay down."

"No, I'm Buster Back Again. I'm Buster the Unbustable for today!" shouted Michael. He grabbed a talc bomb from his knapsack and lobbed it toward Chris. It didn't go anywhere near the fort. Chris caught it neatly in his bare hands.

Meanwhile, Becky took aim and squirted Michael right in the face. "So much for Buster the Unbustable!" she said.

Chris grinned at her. "Good aim!" he shouted.

"The homeguard will triumph!" shouted Becky. She turned and squirted Michael again for good measure. Ashley had tried to sneak through behind Michael, but Becky turned quickly and got Ashley on the arm. Nobody ever said that Becky didn't have great reflexes.

"Atta girl, Becky!" shouted Chris.

"Chris, you and I, we make the best team!" shouted Becky.

I had heard enough. So people thought that I wasn't a fighter. I would show them.

I grabbed one of the talc bombs and dashed in. "Let's go," I said to Lauren. "We can get Chris and Becky if we both go in together."

"The point is supposed to be to get the fort, not them," said Lauren, but she followed me.

I swung the talc bomb over my head, and the next thing I knew I was making the same *"Yee-yee-yee . . . o"* sound that Michael had made. Up till now I had been feeling progressively more down as Chris seemed to be slipping slowly into Becky's web. Now, at least, I could yell at the top of my lungs. I yelled again. I felt better for the first time in days.

I dashed down the hill. I didn't look for the white lines of the fort. All I looked for was Chris and Becky. I saw them duck behind a tree.

"Got ya!" I shouted as I dumped the talc bomb all over their heads.

Meanwhile, I felt something wet dripping down my side.

Then Becky zapped me again with her squirt gun, making mud puddles of my face.

Chris tried to brush the talc off his face.

Meanwhile, Lauren kept her eye on the goal. She was sneaking up on the fort.

"Watch Lauren!" shouted Chris. He went after her with the squirt gun, but his gun was empty. Chris tackled Lauren around the ankle and grabbed the talc bomb away from her.

"Is that fair?" wailed Lauren.

The counselor in charge of the homefort was laughing. "I've never seen any rule against it. Sorry, commandos, this fort is safe. You've got to get striped. I would have to say that this skirmish goes to the homeguard."

Lauren dragged herself up from the mud.

"What happened?" she asked.

"We lost that round," I admitted.

"I told you, Chris. We're unbeatable!" said Becky.

Chris just grinned. I wanted to talc them both.

13

Take No Prisoners

"Michael Buster," said Sweet Willie. "Four stripes already." He painted four purple stripes on Michael's arm. Michael looked down at his arm proudly.

"I earned these stripes, man," said Michael. "Besides, I had a great time!"

Dad painted a stripe on Heidi's arm.

"We all got striped," said Lauren glumly, as she held out her arm to be painted.

"Hey, Lauren, it's an honor to be striped!" said Michael. "Any commando who doesn't get striped is a yellow-bellied worm. We don't have any yellow-bellied worms under my command."

"We didn't come close to capturing the fort,"

said Lauren. "We've gotten lots of glory, but no direct hits."

"Hey, pipsqueak," said Michael. "I'm in command here."

I shook my head. Nobody calls Lauren "pipsqueak" and gets away with it. Michael hadn't even seen how tough Lauren can be in gymnastics. I know Lauren. But to my surprise, Lauren didn't fight him back.

"Where's Ti An?" she asked.

"Talk about pipsqueaks," said Michael, "that little kid stayed out of the battle. She didn't get hit once. She hasn't earned a stripe."

"Have you seen her, Darlene?" asked Lauren.

I wasn't paying attention. Becky and Chris were admiring each other's stripes from when I had hit them with the talc bomb. Chris laughed at something that Becky said.

"Darlene," repeated Lauren, "have you seen Ti An?"

"Not since the first battle started," I said. It was hard not to look at Becky and Chris. The two of them left the Main House and started up the hill toward the gymnastics tent. I couldn't take my eyes off them.

"I wonder where Ti An is," said Lauren.

"Forget her," said Michael. "We've got to make plans for our next assault. This time, we'll try to take them from all angles. We'll bombard them with so many talc bombs they won't know what hit them. Heidi and I will try to take out Chris. Darlene, you proved that you've got some guts."

Michael seemed to be implying he was surprised that I had guts, but I surprised myself — I was flattered anyway. I smiled at him. "Okay, what do you want me to do, Chief?"

"You take out Becky on the next run," he said.

"I don't think Darlene will mind that assignment," said Ashley.

"I thought the object was to get one of our talc bombs *inside* the fort," said Lauren.

"So?" asked Michael belligerently.

"Well, with your plan you've got nobody actually trying to get into the center of the fort. You're just trying to get the defenders."

"It's the *way* the game is played," insisted Michael.

"I know a losing strategy when I see it," said Lauren. She tugged on my arm. "I'm worried about Ti An," she said.

I looked around. I couldn't see Ti An anywhere. "We'll look for her," I said. "After we unload as many talc bombs on Becky's head as we can."

"That is not the object of the game," complained Lauren.

"Maybe not," I shrugged. "But it sure will be

fun. *Yee-yee-yee-o!*" I shouted. "Come on, commandos. We will take no prisoners!"

Lauren gave me a funny look.

"That's the spirit," shouted Michael. He swung a talc bomb in the air just for show and it exploded all over him and me.

"Great! Now you're bombing yourself," said Lauren. "You just wasted a bomb."

Michael was laughing as he shook the talc off him. He looked like a creature from outer space, a mixture of mud and talcum powder.

"CHARGE!" he yelled. Heidi took off with him.

"He doesn't even know where he's going," complained Lauren, huffing after him.

"Who cares?" I said as I charged after him.

"Wait — " said Lauren. She didn't get a chance to finish her sentence.

We got halfway up the knoll toward the gymnastics tent when suddenly we were attacked with homeguard squirt guns. Heidi got hit first, then Michael got tagged.

Becky got me again. Chris stood like somebody from an old western, cocking his gun straight at me. There were homeguards in the trees. It was a total wipeout.

I screamed for the other commandos to take cover, but it was too late.

"Shoot," I said as we had to go back to the

Main House to get striped again. "The gymnastics tent was a perfect place for a homeguard ambush," I admitted.

"That's what I was trying to tell you," said Lauren.

Sweet Willie was laughing. "Michael Buster, that's your last stripe. I think you're going to win some kind of award for foolhardy playing of the game."

"I can still help them plan strategy," said Michael.

"What strategy?" demanded Lauren. "All you've done is get us squirted and got Ti An lost."

"Lauren does have a point," I said. "She should have showed up."

"I don't know," said Lauren. "I am worried about her. All you're worried about is charging after Becky and Chris."

"That's not fair," I protested, but I knew she was right.

Lauren just scowled at me. "And all you care about is showing off to Chris."

"Hey, Lauren," I said, "it's only a game. We'll let you plan the next attack, okay?"

"Yeah," said Michael. "Let's hear your plan, Lauren."

"I can't even think about a plan until we know where Ti An is. She could be lost."

"She's probably playing it safe," said Michael.

"Maybe she's gone AWOL . . . absent without leave. It's the coward's way."

"Ti An is not a coward," said Lauren. She looked to me to stick up for Ti An, and normally I would have, except just then I heard Becky's high-pitched yell. The homeguard was making a sneak attack on another commando's weapon cache.

"Darlene!" yelled Lauren, but I was a commando. I ran to help the other commandos, and I got squirted halfway there in another ambush.

"That's your fourth stripe," said Becky's friend Chelsea triumphantly.

Lauren looked furious. "Can't you tell that Becky has all her friends gunning for you?" she said insistently. "Becky only cares about one thing: showing you up. And you're acting like some macho queen and falling right into her clutches."

Lauren followed me up to the mess hall where I got my fourth stripe. Dad gave me a kind of funny look when he painted it on me.

"One more and you're out," he said.

"Dad, I think I know that," I said with a sigh.

Lauren was pacing up and down on the front porch when I came back from being striped.

"Hey," I said to her. "I'm still not out of it. Don't be so glum."

"It's Ti An," said Lauren. "She still isn't

around. I thought maybe she had been hit and would come up to the mess hall to be striped, but she isn't here."

Lauren looked genuinely worried, and suddenly I started to worry, too.

Trail of Pinecones

Michael and the other commandos were down by the trout pond. Michael was down on one knee drawing a complicated pattern with x's and o's in the dirt with a stick. "Have you seen Ti An?" I asked him.

He ignored my question. "I've got our next attack all planned out," he said.

"Oh, great," muttered Lauren.

"No, this is a good one," said Heidi. "It's a football ploy. We send in a couple of decoys."

"I know all about football," I said. It was funny — at the beginning of the summer I was worried about all the attention I might get just for being Big Beef's daughter. That didn't turn out to be a problem at all. Instead, Becky was my problem. I had been blindsided, as my dad would say in football. Maybe my friends were right, and Chris didn't know that I cared. Somehow after the game, I'd have to find a way to tell him that wasn't true. I did care. I didn't want him to like Becky more than me.

"Darlene," said Michael, "keep your mind on the game. You're going to be a prime decoy."

I'd have plenty of time to make it up to Chris afterward; now I had to concentrate on getting back at Becky. What better way than to wipe out the homeguard!

"Okay, show me the plan," I said.

"Darlene," grumbled Lauren, "what about Ti An? I stuck my head in the bunk. She wasn't there. She isn't anywhere."

"Stop worrying about her," said Michael. "Maybe she just hooked up with another commando team. She could have decided we play too rough. We've gotten more stripes than any other commando team."

"More stripes, and we haven't come close to a fort," said Lauren. "Ti An wouldn't just join up with another team. Ti An is the most loyal kid we know."

"Lauren's right," I said to Michael. "It's not like Ti An to just wander off. She's a team player.

Maybe she's really lost. We should look for her before we do anything else."

"Look, she's a big kid. She can take care of herself."

"She's *not* a big kid, Michael," I protested. "She's only nine years old. Just a little while ago, you were calling her a pipsqueak."

"I'm sure she's not lost. At the end of the game, she'll show up just fine. And we can't lose any time worrying about her," said Heidi.

"What's more important than finding Ti An?" urged Lauren.

"The game," said Heidi without hesitating.

Lauren and I looked at each other.

Heidi knew she had gone too far. She came up to us. "Come on," she urged. "Michael's finally come up with a good plan. You want to show up Becky, don't you?" she whispered to me. "Nothing will impress Chris more than if you win. He pretends to be laid back but, remember, he's my brother."

I knew Heidi was right. Chris and Heidi both liked winners. Still, I couldn't just forget about Ti An. Lauren was biting her thumbnail.

"Maybe we should tell the counselors she's missing," I suggested.

"I don't want her to get in trouble," said Lauren. "Sweet Willie warned us against going off by ourselves. Shouldn't we just look for her for a bit?"

"Where did Ti An hide her talc bombs?" I asked.

"She hid them all along the river when we went on the raft trip," said Lauren.

The trout pond was connected to the river. I walked a few steps and then I spotted something.

"Look at this!" I shouted. It was a pinecone dipped in talc. "It's got to be a clue from Ti An," I said.

"So somebody spilled talc over a pinecone," said Michael. "Who cares?"

"We're the Pinecones," I said.

"You're a commando, not a Pinecone," said Michael. "You're still under my command."

I shook my head. "I was a Pinecone first," I said. "We Pinecones look out for each other."

"Don't give me that one-for-all-and-all-for-one nonsense," said Michael. "We're in the middle of an important game here. We need you to win."

"I've got to find out if Ti An's okay," I said. I looked at Heidi. "Are you coming with us, or are you staying with the commandos?"

Heidi made a face. "I'm sure Ti An's okay," she grunted.

"Fine," I said. "You and Michael and the other commandos go on with your attack. Lauren and

I will try to find Ti An. As soon as we do, we'll rejoin you."

"The game could be over by then," warned Michael.

"Ti An left this pinecone for a reason," I said. "If we don't find her, I'll tell my dad."

"I think you're being silly," said Heidi. "Why not let the counselors worry about her?"

"Look, another white pinecone," said Lauren. "It wasn't an accident. This one's dipped in talc, too."

"Great," said Michael sarcastically. "So your little Pinecone is playing 'Hansel and Gretel.' Those pinecones lead away from the main action. Nothing's happening over there."

Michael had a point. We could hear the shrieks of other commando teams. All the excitement was in the opposite direction. We were going to miss all the fun.

"Hey, here's another one," said Lauren. "I think if we follow the trail of pinecones, we'll find Ti An."

"So what? We won't win the game that way," protested Heidi.

"You don't have to come," I said. "We'll go look for her ourselves."

"Yeah, and when we capture the supersecret fort, you won't get any of the credit," said Michael. "Only the commandos who actually carry out the raid get to have the trophy."

I spotted another pinecone in a stand of aspen trees, leading deeper into the woods and away from the action.

"Good luck," I said to Michael. "We've *got* to try to find Ti An."

"You're crazy," said Michael. Heidi moved away from Michael and over to my side.

"Where are *you* going?" Michael asked.

"I've got to help them," said Heidi.

"You're all nuts," said Michael.

"No, we're not," I said. "We're just Pinecones."

A Bird in the Bush

Every few feet we continued to find pinecones dipped in talc. Unfortunately the trail led through a forest of Colorado blue spruce and there must have been a zillion pinecones on the ground. Sometimes it was hard to pick out the white ones, but if we looked hard enough we always found the next one.

"I don't get it," Heidi complained. "She can't be lost. If she were lost, she could just follow her own pinecone trail back to camp."

"Maybe a bear grabbed her," said Lauren.

I shook my head. "Right, she's being carried off by a bear who just happens to stop every few feet to let her dip a pinecone in talcum powder, and then he picks her up and carries her off again."

"Well, you were the one who said these pinecones had to be a sign from Ti An," said Heidi.

"They are," I said. "I just can't figure out what they mean." Slowly the trail started to climb up. At first the climb was relatively easy, but then it got steeper and steeper. We were following the path of an avalanche slide. I could see a ridge above us. Lauren and Heidi carried their knapsacks filled with talc bombs. It was hard to breathe, the climb was so steep, but still every few feet there was a white pinecone.

"How did she keep the pinecones from sliding down the hill?" said Lauren, huffing up behind me.

"She carefully put them between two rocks," I said. "That blows your bear theory."

"Why did Ti An come up here?" said Heidi, sounding very annoyed.

"She must have had a good reason," I said. "At least I hope so." Below us we could still hear shouts from the game. I wanted so badly to be back down there, showing Chris that I could beat him. I wanted to teach both Becky and Chris a lesson. Instead I was stuck up here following powdered pinecones.

We came out on the same plateau where I had found my gooseberry patch. I could see the white mulberry tree where Becky had first dismounted.

"I didn't know we were so close to camp when I went riding here," I said.

I heard a bird in a nearby gooseberry bush whistle a strange *shee, shh, shee* sound.

"What a funny bird song," I said.

"What bird song?" asked Lauren.

"Listen," I said.

The bird went *"shee, shh, shee"* again. The leaves of the bush shook in the wind. Only there wasn't any wind.

"Maybe it's a rattlesnake," said Heidi.

"There are no rattlesnakes at this altitude," said Lauren. "It's a proven fact."

"It's also a proven fact that rattlesnakes don't go *'shee. . . .'* "

Suddenly I spotted a pair of pigtails growing out of the bush.

"Bushes don't wear pigtails," I whispered.

Ti An crawled out from under the bush. "Will you guys be quiet!" she whispered.

"Ti An!" shouted Lauren. Ti An clapped her hand over Lauren's mouth.

"Shh!" she warned. She sounded just like the bird.

"We thought you were lost," I whispered. Ti An shook her head, indicating that she couldn't talk. She pointed to a huge granite boulder about fifty feet away.

She crawled on her belly toward the boulder.

I shrugged and dropped down onto the ground. I made a motion with my hand to tell Heidi and Lauren to follow me.

When we got to the boulder, Ti An crouched behind it. She peeked up over the top. "I think it's safe to talk here," she whispered. "Did you find my pinecones?"

I nodded.

"I didn't dare leave my lookout," Ti An whispered.

"What lookout?" asked Heidi.

"Be quiet!" said Ti An. "They might move the fort again."

"What fort?" I whispered. "I don't see anything."

Ti An pointed to herself and then to me. I could tell she wanted me to follow her. She got on her stomach and started to crawl on her belly back toward the gooseberry bush, moving herself along with her elbows.

I got down and followed her, even though I knew I was ruining my clothes. When we got near the gooseberry bush, Ti An took a long stick that she pushed along the ground. She raised the stick a couple of inches, and I could see the piece of camouflaged string.

"The supersecret fort!" I started to exclaim. Ti An had her finger to her lips. She pointed. I could see someone guarding it close by. We crawled back to the granite boulder.

"Ti An found the secret fort," I said excitedly. "It's right there by the gooseberry bush. Unfortunately, all my hidden talc bombs are also inside the fort."

"I saw Chris and Becky sneak off in the middle of the battle," said Ti An. "I couldn't find any of you guys to tell you I was going to follow them."

I felt a little guilty. "I was too busy trying to prove what a macho character I was to Chris," I admitted.

"Well, you're going to get your chance now," said Ti An. "It's just Chris and Becky. I saw them a few minutes ago. They're armed with fresh squirt guns."

"Do you have any talc bombs left?" I asked Ti An.

Ti An shook her head. "I used them all up leaving the trail for you."

"I've got two in my knapsack," said Lauren.

"I've got one," said Heidi.

"I don't have any," I confessed. "I used all of mine up, except for the ones that are hidden right in their fort."

"We can't get at those without tipping them off that we're here," said Lauren. "And we have only three talc bombs between us. That's not enough to fight them."

"It will be if I create a diversion," I said. "Becky wants me out of the game more than anything. One more stripe and she gets her wish. If I climb up above their fort and make a lot of noise coming down on them, you can sneak in from the back, get my talc bombs, and drop them in the bull's-eye. Even if they get one of you, the others should be able to do it."

"But it means you'll be out of the game," said Lauren.

"It means we'll win," I said.

16

Fraternizing
with the Enemy

I worked my way up onto a boulder above the fort. I could see Chris and Becky stalking the perimeter. I stepped on a pinecone, and that gave me an idea. Pinecones had worked for Ti An. They could work for me, too.

I grabbed a fistful and started to throw them as hard as I could toward the fort.

Chris looked up first.

Then Becky spotted me. They both rushed toward the front of the fort.

"We've got to get her," shouted Becky. "She's mine!"

"Yee-yee-yee . . . o!" I screamed.

Becky came forward, her squirt gun at the ready. I ducked as a stream of red dye went over my head. I got down on all fours and crawled through the dirt. After this day nobody could ever say I was afraid to get dirty.

Becky stepped out of the perimeter of the fort to try to squirt me.

I made a feint to my right and then dived to my left. I got into the fort. I had one talc bomb left; I lobbed it over my head, but Chris was ready.

He caught it. Then he grinned at me. He knew I had no ammunition left.

"Get her! Get her!" yelled Becky.

Chris took his gun and aimed it. I smiled up at him.

He sensed a trick, but it was too late. He twirled around, but Ti An, Lauren, and Heidi had found my talc bombs and snuck around to the back of the fort.

Chris twirled and shot at Lauren. Then he squirted Heidi. But Ti An was tiny and quick. She lobbed her talc bomb and *splat!* it hit the bull's-eye!

"We won! We won!" I screamed.

Becky came rushing up. "You should have gotten her! You should have gotten her!" she screamed at Chris.

"Becky, the game's over," said Chris.

"You're a mess," he said to me.

"Thank you," I answered. Chris winked at me. I melted. I really did care for him.

Becky had her hands on her hips. She looked furious. "Chris Ferguson," she yelled, "you're guilty of fraternizing with the enemy."

"I've always liked this particular enemy," said Chris.

Becky glared at me. I felt as if she were daring me to tell Chris that I liked him. But I wasn't taking him away from her. He never belonged to her.

17

Gymnasts Make the Best Commandos

At the awards ceremony by the camp fire that night, our commando team was going to be called up to receive our trophy.

"I can't believe that a team made up of mostly new campers won," said Chelsea.

"It's worse than you think," said Michael proudly. "They did it without me. Of course, Darlene had an advantage."

"What was that?" I asked.

"Your being Big Beef's daughter," said Michael. "You're a girl who knows how to think like a real football player."

I started to glare at him. "I meant that as a compliment," teased Michael.

I laughed. "Thanks," I said. I knew he was just

trying to copy the way my dad talked, and it didn't bother me.

Becky came up. I could tell she was still mad. "You must have cheated," she sniveled. "New campers never win."

"We didn't cheat, Becky," I said. "We won by being true Pinecones."

Becky looked like she wanted to gag. It was a pleasure to make her squirm. Chris patted Becky's arm. "Don't feel bad," he said. "We tried our hardest."

"I wouldn't have minded if anybody else had won," said Becky.

Sweet Willie blew his whistle. "Well, we survived another commando day," he said. "Did everybody have a good time?"

There was a loud yell from all the campers.

"Will the winning commando team come up here?" asked Sweet Willie.

"Come on, Ti An," I said. "Without your trail we would never have won."

We told Sweet Willie to let Ti An hold the trophy. It was almost as big as she was.

We sang some camp songs, and Sweet Willie led us in the song "Day is done, gone the sun." It was the signal that we all had to get back to our bunks for lights out.

As we started up the hill toward the bunks, Chris stopped me.

"Congratulations," he said.

"Thanks," I said. "You could have gotten me in the end. Becky really wanted to get me. You and she made a good team."

Chris didn't say anything.

I knew it was up to me. It was time to clear the air. I had been so worried about being embarrassed and about all the gossip, I had forgotten the main point. I *liked* Chris. It wasn't just a competition between Becky and me. "I think you and I make a better team than you and Becky do," I said finally.

Chris looked up at me. "I wasn't sure you felt that way," he said.

"I didn't like being in a position where I had to fight for you," I said.

"I thought you didn't care," said Chris.

"I do," I said. We might have said more but, just our luck, my dad and Sweet Willie were coming up the path. Chris skedaddled. "I'll see you tomorrow, Darlene," he said quickly.

Dad was smiling when he caught up to me. "Congratulations," he said.

"That's just what Chris was saying," I said.

"I bet," said Dad, grinning.

Sweet Willie turned to check on the boys' bunks. "Now, remember, Big Beef, think about what I told you."

Dad walked me toward my bunk. "What was that all about?" I asked him.

"Sweet Willie wants me to become part owner of the camp. Should I do it? Do you think you'd want to come back?"

"Are you kidding?" I said. "I wouldn't miss it. Gymnasts make the best commandos."

About the Author

Elizabeth Levy decided that the only way she could write about gymnastics was to try it herself. Besides taking classes she is involved with a group of young gymnasts near her home in New York City and enjoys following their progress.

Elizabeth Levy's other Apple Paperbacks are *A Different Twist, The Computer That Said Steal Me,* and all the other books in THE GYMNASTS series.

She likes visiting schools to give talks and meet her readers. Kids love her presentations. Why? "I start with a cartwheel!" says Levy. "At least I try to."

WIN A TRIP TO THE
1991
WORLD GYMNASTICS CHAMPIONSHIPS

We'll send the Winner of this random drawing and his/her parent or guardian (age 21 or older) to the exciting 1991 WORLD GYMNASTICS CHAMPIONSHIPS in Indianapolis, Indiana! The trip includes:

★ Hotel — 3 nights! (September 13, 14 and 15, 1991)
★ Round-trip airline tickets!
★ 2 premium seat tickets to major championship events!

Just fill in the coupon below and return it by May 31, 1991.

1991 World Gymnastics Championships

Name _____ Age _____

Street _____

City _____ State _____ Zip _____

Where did you buy this *Gymnasts* book?

❑ Bookstore   ❑ Drugstore   ❑ Supermarket   ❑ Library
❑ Book Club   ❑ Book Fair   ❑ Other_____ (specify)

★ GYM790 ★

APPLE PAPERBACKS

THE GYMNASTS™

by Elizabeth Levy